KIMBERLY LEMMING

What's A Girl Gotta Do To Get On The Naughty List

Copyright © 2023 by Kimberly Lemming

All rights reserved. No part of this publication may be reproduced, stored or transmitted in any form or by any means, electronic, mechanical, photocopying, recording, scanning, or otherwise without written permission from the publisher. It is illegal to copy this book, post it to a website, or distribute it by any other means without permission.

This novel is entirely a work of fiction. The names, characters and incidents portrayed in it are the work of the author's imagination. Any resemblance to actual persons, living or dead, events or localities is entirely coincidental.

Kimberly Lemming asserts the moral right to be identified as the author of this work.

First edition

This book was professionally typeset on Reedsy.
Find out more at reedsy.com

Contents

Content Warnings	iv
Chapter 1	1
Chapter 2	13
Chapter 3	27
Chapter 4	33
Chapter 5	42
About the Author	47
Also by Kimberly Lemming	49

Content Warnings

PLEASE BE AWARE: This book contains attempted murder, breaking & entering, degradation, BDSM and sexually explicit content that could trigger certain audiences.

Chapter 1

"Are you going to get into the sack willingly or do I need to start being less polite?" The demon in the doorway was a monstrous thing indeed. Long arcing horns brushed against the popcorn ceiling I used to fantasize about scraping smooth. He stepped further inside, his hooves clacked against the wood floor as they left the cushion of the snowman themed welcome mat I'd picked out only a month ago. He shrugged off the red sack he carried and opened it wide, gesturing for me to get in.

My fist squeezed around the box cutter I hid behind my back, unsure if I'd have to use it on him or throw it out the window to hide the evidence. I bit the inside of my cheek. This was supposed to be an easy job. Louis and She Who Shall Not Be Named should have been having Christmas Eve dinner at my parents. Did they know what I was planning and hire one of their friends to act as security? Dammit, dammit, dammit!

No, I can't falter here. Not so close to the finish line. I steeled my nerves and straightened my back. Show no fear. "This is you being polite? Last I checked, strangers don't break into homes and order their occupants to get in sacks."

The demon quirked an eyebrow. "Now there's the pot calling the kettle black."

"Um, excuse you, this is my house."

"Oh is it now?"

"Yes, it is." Or at least, it should be. If there was any justice in the world.

"Mmhmm. Is that why you removed the doorknob?" he gestured pointedly to the knob and screwdriver I'd haphazardly dropped in the entryway.

Fuck. He was on to me, but I wouldn't give up. I spent my days arguing with old men in board meetings. If I could convince them to take a chance on hiring our purple-haired, fishnet-wearing social media manager, I could convince this dickhead in an off-brand Halloween costume that I was still well within my rights to be here. There wasn't a situation alive I couldn't gaslight, gatekeep or girlboss my way out of. "Clearly, I'm just replacing the locks."

He sighed, green eyes closing with a disappointed shake of his head. "Daphne, my naughty list is especially long this year. Spare me the theatrics and I might yet show leniency during your punishment."

"Uh, punishment? There will be no punishment of any kind, you weirdo. Just who do you think you are?"

The monster stared, unamused. "The Easter Bunny. Now get in the sack."

I squinted at him, trying to find where the mask ended. Yet the gray fur covering his body looked seamless. There must have been some kind of zipper on the back. "Kalvin, is that you?"

Chapter 1

"I don't know who this Kalvin is, but I assure you, I am not him."

"Yeah, I'm not buying it." Of all of Louis's friends, Kalvin was the one most likely to agree to whatever stupid stunt this was. The enormous frame matched as well. Though, despite the man being built like a quarterback, I didn't remember him being so tall. Looking down, I noticed a pair of hooves where his feet should have been. Ah, that explained the extra height. It was a rather convincing costume, I'll give him that. Still, Louis and The Treacherous One wouldn't get rid of me that easily.

I stalked over to him, rose to my tippy-toes and yanked on his horn. When the mask didn't come off, I gripped the other and gave them both a yank. "Damn, this thing is on tight. Did you glue it to your head or something?"

He reached up and grabbed my wrist to still me. "If you mean to extend your punishment, little one, it's working."

Hmm, the straightforward approach wasn't working. Louis could come home at any minute and I still needed to tidy up for my plan to work. Time to switch gears. "Little one?" I asked, looking him up and down. "I could get used to a name like that." When he didn't push me away, I trailed my fingers along his forearm and flashed what I hoped to god was a seductive smile. "Tell you what, how about I put that lock back, you slip out of this costume and the two of us get out of here and grab a bite? Home projects really work up a girl's appetite."

"And the honeyed words of a liar often stoke mine. Alas, your crimes only just placed you on the naughty list." The smell of crisp peppermint and fresh-cut evergreen flitted past my senses as he leaned down and drew in a breath. I shivered and stepped away, only to feel the press of his large hand on the small off my back. The sharp tips of his claws pricked through the fabric of my sweater, sending a thrill down my spine. "Rest assured, dear one, should you decide to ignore the lesson I teach you tonight, I'll return next Christmas Eve and devour you *entirely*."

He drew his face closer still and I gasped when his hot tongue ran along my neck. "You have the taste of something truly devious about you. Perhaps a year is too long." He leaned back to meet my gaze. The sharp sting of his claw pressed against my lower lip. "Tell me Daphne Cordova, does your mischief only extend to petty vengeance or could I persuade you to do something more depraved?"

I don't remember Kalvin having a voice capable of rendering women into puddles, but here we are. I expected the frat bro turned respectablish accountant to fall at the first fluttered lashes I sent his way. Louis was a jealous man and always kept my hangouts with his friends brief. Maybe he just didn't want me to know about this side of his best friend. Not that it mattered. Fucking one of his best friends hadn't been a part of my master revenge scheme, but the further he pulled me against him, the more brilliant the idea looked.

The bastard fucked my sister after all.

"You make me sound like some hardened criminal." My hands slid around his neck as I leaned into him, boldly pushing my chest against the red fabric of his coat. I felt around the base of his neck for the zipper, then dipped lower when I found none.

"Hardened, no," he chuckled. "Just naughty enough." Pale green eyes searched my own as the tips of black claws traced the curve of my spine. "Tell me, little one, are you ready for your punishment? Or are you still trying to find my zipper?"

My hands froze. Sweat beaded along my neck as I noticed just how real his costume seemed to be. I pushed away from him, nearly toppling over when the back of my knees hit the

Chapter 1

coffee table. "You're not Kalvin, are you?"

The beast shook his head.

"Then who?"

He smiled, showing off rows of sharp teeth. "Didn't I tell you? I'm the Easter Bunny."

"This isn't funny anymore," I spat. "Who are you? What the hell is going on?!"

His eyes closed on an inhale, savoring the air like it was the last breath he'd ever take. "Fear," he purred. "Such fair perfume. Now that I have your attention," he said, sweeping into a bow. "I am the scrape of branches at the window when your guilt begins to fester, the warning mother's whisper to mischievous children and the dark shadow of Old St. Nick." With a lift of his head he said, "You may call me Krampus and you, dear Daphne, are on my naughty list."

All I could say was, "Oh." My hands clapped together as I rocked back on my feet. Plan, what's the plan? Remember our motto, gaslight, gatekeep, girlboss! "Look, Kramps. Can I call you Kramps?"

"I'd rather you didn't."

"You're right," I said, waving a hand. "That was…that was terrible. Anyway, there must be some kind of mistake with your list, you see. I have committed no crimes. And on the off chance I did, which I didn't, there's not a damn chance it was anything bad enough to warrant the dark shadow of Old St. Nick to pay me a visit."

I shuffled around the coffee table, slowly backing my way out of the living room. Each click of his hooves was another icicle lodged in my chest. My foot stepped on the loose floorboard that I'd never been able to convince my Nana to fix. Its squeak slightly dimmed by the cushion of shrimp I'd stashed underneath. And despite the fact that some supernatural hellbeast was looming over me, despite the fact that I *knew* I was being fucking crazy, I still raised my knee high and stomped again and again on that board to make damn sure the harbingers of my malice didn't notice the change in sound before the scent of their new love nest started to *rot*.

"Why don't we review the charges then?" he asked, ignoring my stomping fit.

"By all means."

He pulled back his coat and retrieved a scroll. "Daphne Cordova, the charges against you are as follows: stealing your sister's cat,"

"She's my cat."

He fixed me with a look and I shut my mouth. "You are also accused of keying your ex-fiancé's car,"

"Allegedly," I snapped. "Those charges were dismissed."

"Which brings me to your next charge: obstruction of justice."

I shrugged. "I've no idea what you mean."

Green eyes peered at me from above his scroll. "You slept with the judge in order to have the case dismissed."

"No, I slept with the judge because he looked like Winston Duke. Last time I checked, sexiness wasn't a crime."

"It is when it hampers the judicial system."

"Well, Louis slept with my sister!"

"Did it cause a judge to throw out a case? No? Moving on. Next, we have vandalism and, of course, breaking and entering." He looked pointedly at the doorknob on the floor. Then he reached for the wicker basket on his back and pulled out a gnarled birch branch.

"Whoa, whoa, wait a minute," I said, throwing my arms up. "All of that must be some kind of misunderstanding. There's no

Chapter 1

need to do...whatever it is you wanna do with that thing."

"Is that right?" His slow advance mirrored my stumbling retreat.

"Yes! There's a lot of extenuating circumstances you don't know about."

"Excuses will get you nowhere, Dear One."

"Not *excuses*, extenuating circumstances. If you could just give me a moment to explain." Wilted mint leaves brushed against my shoulder as I backed into the kitchen. I bit my cheek to avoid taking my eyes off the beast to check the state of Nana's herb garden. The one She Who Shall Not Be Named swore up and down she knew how to take care of, just to fuck me over from receiving anything in the house.

Yet my eyes drifted to sickly yellow leaves and my heart squeezed around memories of morning tea and gossip. "Fuck, hold on." The water can was in my hand before I even gave him a chance to respond. He watched in stunned silence as I quickly watered the wilting plants and dropped a few squirts of plant food into the fussy mint.

"Alright," I began, placing the water can back on the shelf. "As I said, I did not steal my sister's cat. Freeloader was my Nana's cat and she was left to me when Nana passed. This whole house and everything in it was, to be exact. So, as you can see, there's no way I could be guilty of breaking and entering. Or any of those other charges, really."

"Your Nana may have meant to leave you these possessions at some point, but it seems her will was changed just before she passed-"

"Because that bitch cornered her when she was blissed out on painkillers!" I shouted, unable to keep my anger in check. "I refused to follow the order of a judge that didn't give a damn that the will was changed while Nana couldn't even remember who was who. You want to punish someone truly evil, go after my twin!"

"Really?" the beast asked. "You're pulling the evil twin card?"

"Because Charlotte is evil! She's been the golden child all her life. It killed her to think I was getting married before her and getting Nana's house. Although I was the one living here and taking care of her. Charlotte never lifted a finger or drove her to a single appointment. Yet I'm supposed to believe Nana signed everything over to her at the last minute? Fuck no! I don't even care that she ruined my engagement. She can have Louis. That sniveling backstabber isn't worth the tears, but this is MY house. Shouldn't you know all of this? I mean, you somehow knew I was breaking in here, right?"

Krampus paused, then lowered his branch. He retrieved a phone from his pocket and held up a finger for me to wait. For some reason, the sight of the completely normal device in this monster man's hand threw me for a loop. I guess there was no rule about mythical creatures not being able to use technology, but still. Did Santa have a phone? I wanted to know his data plan.

The person on the other end answered on the first ring. "Who had eyes on Charlotte Cordova?" he asked. A muscle ticked in his jaw at the muffled reply. "Fucking interns." He moved past me to take a seat at the breakfast nook, then waved a hand at the other side. "Alright, you have my attention. Explain."

"I-really?" I blinked. Then quickly snapped out of my shock and pulled out my phone, already itching to regale anyone who would listen to the clusterfuck that had been my year. It didn't take long to find the cloud folder full of receipts of their transgressions. I had it bookmarked after all. "Do you

Chapter 1

want anything to drink? This could take a minute."

The beast leaned back in his chair and shrugged. "Does your evil twin have any eggnog?"

Grinning, I retrieved a pair of glasses from the cabinet and raided the fridge for eggnog and pecan pie. Then noticed - with no small irritation - that Charlotte had already started rearranging the cabinets into her god-awful way. Who puts plates in the lower cabinets instead of the pots and pans? Heathens, that's who.

I beat down the dinnerware rant building in my throat and set our food and drinks at the table before sliding into the booth. Krampus nodded in thanks and helped himself to the first bite of pie. "Alright, get comfy monster man, this one's a doozy."

"I'm all ears," he said, sipping his eggnog. Some of it dribbled down his chin. His tongue unfurled and I swear on my life the world slowed like in a cheesy teen movie when the "ugly" secretly pretty girl walks in without her glasses. It was a deep red and long enough to swipe the offending eggnog off his chin. A row of metal ball piercings lining the center commanded all of my attention as that tongue slid down to his throat to catch the last drop of liquid.

I dropped my fork. I dropped my jaw. I dropped every thought in my mind that didn't involve a row of metal beads flicking against my dirtiest dreams. What, exactly, was his punishment? I may have reacted hastily.

Krampus swallowed and set his cup down. "Are you alright?"

"Huh?" I blinked rapidly, then looked down at my plate to avoid staring at the horns that were starting to look a lot like handlebars. "I mean...yes. I'm fine, where...where was I?"

"Your evil twin?"

"Yes! Of course." I fumbled around for my phone and pulled

up the original will. I started from the beginning, from growing up with the monster our parents' favoritism created, to finding her and Louis in my bed weeks before our wedding and the hell I went through when I found out that Charlotte had manipulated Nana into signing everything over to her while she was barely conscious enough to remember her own name. He listened to my tale of woe without interruption. Krampus silently checked over the copy of Nana's medical evaluation the judge ignored when I tried to fight the false will.

When I finished, he set the phone down and asked, "I have to know: how does the shrimp play into all this?"

"Right. Well, this is probably going to sound crazy, but I had this plan where I hide shrimp throughout the house. In a few weeks it will start to rot and stink up the place. Worst-case scenario, I ruin Louis and Charlotte's new love nest. Best-case scenario, they abandon it completely and I can move back in. So long as I didn't get caught, it seemed like an easy win for me."

Krampus laughed and shook his head. "I need to make another call," he said, rising from his seat.

"Wait," I called, grabbing his hand. "Does this mean you believe me?"

He took my hand and squeezed and the level of comfort in that small touch rocked me to my core. "I believe you. Wait here."

I believe you. Fuck, how long had I been waiting for someone to say that? Tears pricked my eyes as I watched him retreat out the back door. I sat at the table, trying to pull myself together. For months I had no one in my corner - aside from my friends at least. Even my own parents just tried to convince me to let it go in order to keep the peace. They always said Charlotte was

Chapter 1

the sensitive one and had to come first. They justified going along with the new will and giving her the house because I made more money than her. They dismissed the fact that she and Louis ripped my heart out of my chest because 'you can't help who you love.' Then they acted like I was the crazy one when I refused to sit across from my cheating ex and my bitch of a sister for a nice family Christmas Eve dinner. They never even bothered to try and listen. But, this monster of all things, did. He believed me.

How fucked up is that?

When Krampus returned, I snapped out of my musing. He slumped into his seat with a thud, then reached into his wicker basket and pulled out a bottle of brandy. He uncorked it and poured a generous helping into my empty glass, then filled his own.

"You just keep a full bottle of brandy in your basket? A man after my own heart."

"It's no snickerdoodle martini, but it gets the job done."

"I'm sorry, snickerdoodle martini? Where do I get one of those?"

"The elves at Santa's workshop make drinks you'd weep over. Play your cards right and maybe they'll bring you one for Christmas." Krampus lifted his cup and gestured for me to do the same. When I did, he clinked them together with a cheers and threw it back.

"What did I just cheers to?" I asked, drinking mine as well.

He grinned. "Daphne Cordova, rejoice. You are the first person in history to be removed from my naughty list."

"That's great!" I said, standing up. "Does that mean I can get back to stuffing shrimp in hard-to-find places?"

"Oh no," he laughed. "I've got something much more fitting

in mind. Run along before they return."

"What? Absolutely not. If you plan on punishing them, I want to stick around for the show."

He gave me a smile that had my pulse racing. "Bloodthirsty little creature, aren't you? Unfortunately for you, I am no entertainer. Begone, lest you wish to feel the bite of my branches yourself."

The combination of brandy and eggnog must have muddled my sense of decency. Otherwise I would have never found myself saying, "The bite of a branch might be a hard limit for me, but if it means I get my revenge, I'd be open to the sting of your claws."

One corner of his mouth pulled into a slight grin. "Have another drink," he said, refilling my glass. "You'll need it."

"Fuck yes!"

Chapter 2

It probably said a lot about me that the moment before I was about to scare the ever-living shit out of my sister was the happiest I'd been in months. But I'll work that out in therapy later. Tonight, an icy wind howled the song of vengeance through bare branches and to me it carried the tune of a Christmas miracle.

As car lights pulled into the driveway, I cast a glance at my partner in crime, only to find the space beside me empty. Shit, did he leave? "Krampus?" I whispered.

His deep voice sounded all around me, making me jump. "I'm still here. Are you ready to take your spot?"

"Yeah, what do I do?" No sooner had the words left my mouth than my body dissolved into mist. "WHAT THE F-" My sentence was cut off when my mouth disappeared. The world shifted and I got the feeling of being thrown toward the wall before everything snapped into place again. I looked around to see delicately painted rose bushes. My own hands looked painted on as well. Except with a lot more wrinkles than

I remembered. "What just happened?"

"I've hidden you inside your grandmother's painting. Now, stay quiet until I give you the signal."

"YOU CAN DO THA-"

"Shh."

"Right, right. I'm cool, I'm focused." Keys jingled just outside the door as Louis fumbled with the lock. I relaxed into my position in Nana's rocking chair and folded my hands in my lap, doing my best to imitate the pose. Judging by the slurred words and giggles coming from the entryway, Charlotte and Louis were probably too tipsy to notice anything amiss.

"Was the doorknob always upside down?" Louis asked.

Whoops.

Charlotte snorted before jiggling the lock open and stepping inside. "Must have been the repair man. I just called the first guy available so I could get the locks changed ASAP. You know how bitter Daphne is."

Louis stumbled into the dimly lit foyer after her, wrapping his arms around her waist with a laugh. "She'll get over it, eventually. Not much she can do now that she's lost the lawsuit, anyway." He took her by the hand and spun her around.

Charlotte brought a hand up to stifle her giggles. "Still, it's too bad she chickened out of dinner. I would have paid good money to see her face when we told my parents we're engaged." She lifted her hand with a triumphant smirk, admiring the rock on her hand. Even from a distance, I'd recognize that sapphire centerpiece anywhere. It was my ring. Well, the one I threw at Louis's head after I found him balls deep inside her, but still.

That. Fucking. *Bitch.*

Rage boiled my blood and I damn near leapt out of the painting for a good old fashioned sister smackdown. I felt

Chapter 2

the presence of brawny arms wrap around my waist, stilling me.

Krampus leaned into me from behind and his body shifted as if made of dark smoke. He looked nearly transparent, but his hold on me was firm. "Be silent," he whispered against my temple. "You'll spoil the fun."

There's that damn panty dropping voice again. I pressed my legs together and tried to fight the overwhelming need to turn my face into his neck and breathe in that peppermint evergreen scent. He moved his lips to my ear before he faded into nothingness. "Watch how it's done."

I couldn't help but grin when the door slammed shut on its own. Charlotte jumped with a shriek, clinging to Louis's arm. "It's just the wind," Louis said with a laugh.

"That wind nearly had me jumping out of my skin," she breathed. The lights flickered and she cursed. "This damn old house. It's just one thing after another. I'm half tempted to just sell it and be done."

Louis collected her in his arms. "Don't be like that. A bit of new wiring, some paint and the place will be good as new. Next week we can start getting rid of your Nana's things. Right now, this place looks like a depressed nursing home."

"It is very grandma chic," she agreed. Charlotte plucked an old family photo from the wall and curled her lip. With a flick of her wrist, the picture was tossed into the trash bin. "We'll start with these god-awful picture frames."

All at once, every photo was sent tumbling to the floor, their clattering echoed through the quiet house. Charlotte froze, her eyes widening in unease. She peered at the painting I was in, the only thing that remained in place and swallowed thickly.

Louis rubbed the back of his neck, the way he always did when he was nervous or lying. Or nervous about lying. "Must be a draft in here or something." The last of his words came out in visible puffs as the temperature plummeted. Ornaments jingled on the Christmas tree and their shadows danced. Krampus made the flights flicker again and each flash of light morphed the shadows into grotesque monsters that crept along the walls. I reveled in the terror that crept across Charlotte's face.

"That's not a fucking draft Louis, what the hell is going on?" she asked.

"Don't panic, I'm sure it's-" His words cut off with the lights. Charlotte screamed. Static crackled from the radio before jingle bells started to play. Its cheery melody felt deeply out of place with the sinister chill in the air.

Dashing through the snow
In a one-horse open sleigh

"I'm getting the fuck out of here," Charlotte said. Her hands fumbled in the dark, searching for the keys she'd dropped in the entryway.

"Babe, it's nothing!"

O'er the fields we go
*Laughing all the way, ha **ha ha***

The song's laughter bled into a malevolent cackle before the music halted. The lights flashed on just as tinsel from the Christmas tree wrapped around Louis's legs. He fell to the ground with a scream. His hands tore at the tinsel, frantically calling for my sister, who stood frozen in fear. He was cocooned in seconds.

With a bang, the front door burst open. Cold air blasted through the room, nearly sending Charlotte to the floor. Christmas lights unwound themselves from the porch and started to drag Louis out of the house. Charlotte screamed

Chapter 2

and flattened herself against the wall, far out of reach. Colorful lights flashed as Louis's screaming cocoon was dragged outside. The door slammed shut with a click of its lock.

"Shit, shit!" Charlotte moved to open the door, but it was sealed shut. Desperate, she banged against it, screaming for help.

With a gentle tug, Krampus pulled me from the painting. I found myself consumed by dark magic. I caught a glimpse of my reflection in the window and saw the spectral vision of my Nana staring back at me. The transformation was disorienting, and I could feel the aching weight of age settle into my bones.

He pushed softly at my back and whispered, "Time to shine, little one. Make it a show, would you?"

If it's a show he wants, it's a show he'll get. I closed my eyes and pictured my Nana at her fiercest. Before all meds and doctors and grief. She was a force of nature. If she saw the dirty tricks Charlotte had employed to take what she built, there wasn't enough Christmas magic in the world to save her. Spine straight as an oak, head held high with the might of a woman fierce enough to keep her family in check, I stepped forward.

The floorboards creaked beneath my feet and Charlotte whipped around. Her mouth fell open in a silent scream and she staggered backward. I looked down my nose at her and spoke with a voice full of authority, disappointment seeping through every word. "Charlotte Ann Cordova, you've always been a spoiled child, but I expected better of you."

"Nan-"

"Did I give you permission to interrupt?" I asked and my words carried a weight beyond the grave.

"No ma'am," she stammered.

"You defrauded me on my deathbed, you threw your sister out

of the house I left her and for what? To lie next to a mediocre bastard?" When Charlotte remained silent, I raised my voice and ordered, "Speak child!"

"I…Nana, how could you know about any of that?"

"Did you think death could stop me? I always know what's going on in my family and you, child, have been very naughty."

Krampus stepped from the shadows of the foyer and his massive form loomed over her. With a bone-chilling rumble he asked, "Are you ready for your punishment?"

Charlotte's face turned ashen as she stared up at him. She fell back on her ass, nails clawing at the wall behind her as if she meant to tear through it to freedom. "I'll fix it!" she bellowed. "I'll fix everything! I'll transfer the house to Daphne, she can have Louis, the ring, anything!"

I held her gaze, letting the terror seep into her marrow before giving a final, spine-chilling command, "Get out."

Charlotte was a track star in her youth, yet I'd never seen her run faster. She tripped over Louis, who had only just freed himself from the tinsel and the couple ran screaming to their car and drove off into the night, nearly crashing into the mailbox as they went.

Krampus closed the door and the house itself seemed to exhale. A quick glance at my reflection proved that his magic had faded as quickly as it came.

No, that's not quite right. The magic of his illusions had faded into the night, yet the air still singed like a crackle of lightning just before the storm. For the second time that night, I found myself staring up at the monster silhouetted in my foyer. He stood motionless, his hand still pressed to the door as if he didn't dare turn to face me. His sharp green eyes seemed to glow as he peered at me over his shoulder.

Chapter 2

For a moment, nothing happened. A shiver rolled up my spine and I couldn't tell if it was from fear or want or both. For the sake of the Christmas spirit, I'm just gonna go with both.

Then his hand left the door and the crackle of magic in the air sizzled through me until my body felt coiled like a spring.

Eyes hungry, he moved closer. His large body dwarfed my own as he gazed down at me. A crooked smile pulled at his lips. "It's not too late, little one. I won't stop you from backing out now." Krampus searched my face and he must have liked what he saw. He took my chin in his hand and leaned down to trace his lips along my jaw. "But that's not what you want, is it? I could taste it, you know. How much you relished punishing those who wrong you. Your blood practically sang with malice." He leaned away and settled a possessive hand around my neck. "But it's not enough, is it?"

Trembling hands wove into the gray ruff of his neck as I stared up at him. He was right; it wasn't enough by a long shot. My eyes closed and I tried to steady the tremor in my voice as I forced out the words. "I-I've never been a bad girl."

The rumble of his chest sounded more animal than man. "I don't believe that for a second."

My pulse quickened as his clawed hand tightened around my throat. His other hand slid along the curve of my waist. He dragged his claws along my thigh, sliding underneath my skirt until I felt them trace along the delicate fabric of my panties. My eyes fluttered open and the heat in his gaze sent a rush of warmth to pool between my thighs.

"Tell me, have you ever fantasized about taking a little something that didn't belong to you? Or perhaps, seeking revenge before this?"

I swallowed and wet my lips. "Perhaps. If the opportunity

arose."

"Then you've never had a chance to really be wicked." His thumb brushed against my lower lip. "And you're just the sort of depraved little thing to jump at the first chance."

His hands moved to my hips. My heart hammered in my chest as he lifted me. He held me pinned against the wall, his cock hard and thick against my thigh. He nuzzled my neck and nipped at the soft skin below my ear. I gasped and the sound made his cock jump.

"You've been such a good girl, Daphne," he purred. "Such a perfect little rule follower until tonight. But I know the truth." His hips rocked against mine, his teeth nipped at my neck. "I can smell the corruption on you. It's delicious."

Sliding his hand from my neck down to my chest, he gripped the front of my shirt and tore it from my body. My nipples pebbled in his hand. When he left my neck to suck on the rigid flesh, I shuddered.

Then he bit it. I screamed in pain and pleasure as he ground my nipple between his teeth. I grabbed his shoulders and couldn't control how hard I squeezed them. He stopped biting and licked my nipple with his enormous tongue. I gasped each time one of his piercings collided with my sensitive flesh. He switched to my left breast and nibbled it like he had my right. He kept alternating between them, nibbling, licking and squeezing.

"I can see it now," he whispered, moving his lips to the shell of my ear. "The things you'd do if given a chance. And I can't wait to see it."

My head spun with the possibilities. What kind of punishment could the creature before me come up with? Would he tie me down? Tease me? Spank me?

I didn't care, I wanted it all.

Chapter 2

"Show me," I moaned.

He chuckled, and the sound reverberated through me. Krampus set me down on my feet, then took me by the hand. His hooves clicked against the wood floors, the noise a gentle counterpoint to the hammering in my chest. He led me up the stairs and, with each step, his pace grew quicker. I stumbled to keep up.

When he opened the door to the master bedroom, I nearly choked. Charlotte had already had the place gutted. Every piece of furniture and decoration was gone. In their place stood an elaborate four-poster bed.

Krampus shoved me forward. "You can burn her furniture later, vicious thing. Undress," he commanded.

Shaking, I did as I was told. My hands fumbled with my skirt and the remnants of my tattered sweater, they hit the floor along with my bra and panties.

"Hands and knees."

I crawled onto the bed and waited. The air in the room was warm and it felt like fire licking at my skin.

Krampus circled the bed, his hooves heavy on the wood floor. I could feel the mattress sink where he knelt behind me. His hand came down hard on my ass. The sting surprised me and I cried out.

Groaning, he lavished the stinging flesh with his tongue, the cold metal piercings teased my flesh. "How long have you wanted to punish her, Daphne?"

"I-"

His hand came down again. "Don't lie to me, little one."

"Years," I choked.

Another smack. My pussy clenched around nothing and I couldn't help whimpering at the promise of a monster's cock filling it.

"Do you know why you've been so angry for so long?"

I shook my head.

"You're not a talented liar."

He smacked me again, then took my jaw in his hand and shoved his tongue into my mouth. My pulse throbbed at the rough way he marauded his way deeper, claiming my throat until my knees threatened to buckle. He broke the kiss and I gasped for breath.

"Why have you been so angry?"

"I-I don't know."

Smack.

"Wrong answer. Try again."

I gasped. The heat from his touch seared into my skin. "She took everything."

He chuckled, soothing my bottom in gentle strokes. "But it's not just her, is it? You strike me as the Honor Roll sort. Let me guess, top of your class, highest performer at work, always the one taking charge of everything. You'd do anything for a little recognition, wouldn't you, dear one?"

Smack.

"Yes!"

His fingers teased along my inner thighs. I was dripping wet and I needed him to touch me.

"So desperate for a little attention, aren't you?"

"Yes."

His fingers slipped between my folds and teased along my entrance.

"You're such a needy little slut."

"Please," I begged.

"Say it."

Chapter 2

"I'm a needy slut," I moaned.

He pressed the tip of his finger inside me, his sharp claw nicked at my entrance and a cry left my lips. "Well, this won't do. Can't go marking up my pretty little treat, can I?" Krampus brought his hand to his mouth and bit the claws off three of his fingers, then pressed one inside. "I knew the moment I saw you, I knew you were a depraved little thing just waiting for an excuse. Every promotion they passed you over for, every victory gone unseen, you let that disappointment fester into something darker. Something naughty."

He added a second finger and curled them. They stroked inside me, teasing the sensitive nerves. I gasped and pushed back against his hand, but he pulled away.

"Patience," he whispered, then smacked my ass.

The pain sent a pulse of pleasure to my core.

"I've punished countless naughty mortals, Daphne, but you…"

His fingers pressed into me again and his thumb flicked over my clit. My body clenched.

"You're something special. So wicked and desperate for someone to make you hurt. You've been waiting for the right monster to come along, haven't you?"

"Yes!"

My pussy clenched and my muscles trembled as the pressure built. Just as I reached the precipice, he pulled away, laughing at my indignant whine.

"Beg," he demanded.

"Please," I gasped.

"Please?" he mocked. "Come now, Miss Honor Roll. You can do better than that. Beg!"

"I need it, please."

"Need what?"

"I need your cock," I pleaded.

"What a greedy mortal."

"I need your cock. Please, fuck me. Fuck me, please, I'll do anything."

"Good girl," he whispered. "I will not be gentle," he warned.

"Good! Please just fuck me!"

The head of his cock pressed against my entrance, then slammed into me. I cried out. His hands dug into my hips as he pounded into me. The sharp pricks of his remaining claws dug into my flesh with a burn so fucking delicious I could weep from joy. His hips snapped forward. Pain mixed with pleasure and I screamed.

"That's it," he hissed. "Cry for me." His tongue snaked its way down his body to tease at my bottom. He swirled the first piercing around the ring of tight muscles, then shoved his tongue deep in my ass.

"Fuck!" I was already falling apart and when the second metal ball plundered inside me, I nearly started speaking in tongues.

"Do you want to cum?"

"Yes!"

"Too bad."

His fingers wound through my hair and he pulled my head back. The sudden sting made me yelp.

"I can feel how close you are, naughty girl. Do you think you've earned it?"

"No," I cried.

"No, what?"

"No, sir."

He let go of my hair and his hand came down on my ass. The sting was sharper now and tears stung my eyes.

"So good," he growled. "You're being such a good girl, aren't

Chapter 2

you?"

"Yes, sir."

"You love it when I smack your ass like this, don't you?"

"I do, sir."

"Do you want more?"

"Yes, sir."

"Ask nicely."

"Please, sir." In the far corners of my mind, I couldn't help but wonder how he was still talking while tonguing my ass. Must be another Christmas miracle.

"I don't think so." His fingers dug into the soft flesh of my hips as he slammed into me again and again. "You've been a very bad girl, haven't you, Daphne?"

"Yes, sir."

"You want to be punished."

"Yes, sir."

"How should I punish you, little one?"

"I-I don't know."

His fingers wound in my hair again. "Yes you do," he purred. "How many times did you fantasize about getting revenge on all the people who walked over you? Tell me what you imagined, little one."

"I thought about hurting them. About humiliating them. I'd shave their hair off or slash their tires."

"And?"

"And, I wanted to break them."

"Good girl."

He let go of my hair and moved his hand between my thighs. His thumb grazed over my clit.

"And how would you break them, naughty girl?"

"I'd tie them up. Make them beg for it. I'd tease them,

embarrass them, and then leave them wanting."

"So vicious," he rumbled.

His thrusts slowed as his fingers teased over my clit.

"That's right," he cooed. "Show me what a naughty girl you can be. I want to see the real you."

The pressure built until I was shaking with it.

"That's it, little one. Come for me." The words were a command. One that I obeyed. My body shook as pleasure tore through me.

He pulled out and I felt the sticky warmth of his cum splatter across my back. He was breathing hard and I could hear the pounding of his heart. We lay there together, basking in the afterglow.

Chapter 3

When I woke up alone, I realized I had absolutely no way of contacting Krampus. The man just vanished into the night like the Ghost of Christmas Past. Which, based on the wild dick game he showed last night, was simply unacceptable. How was I supposed to go back to human men after that? I had to find a way to contact him. Even if I had to get back onto the naughty list to do it.

Of course, it had to be teeth chatteringly cold the one Christmas I decided to turn to a temporary life of crime. I hugged my arms around myself, shivering something fierce as I stood outside of Wicked Whisk Bakery. My breath formed puffy clouds in the morning light as I wracked my brain, trying to remember where Daisy kept her damn key. "I could call her, but I guess that completely defeats the purpose of breaking in and getting on the naughty list. Dammit."

I peered through the frost-kissed window, my eyes scanning the darkened interior of the bakery. "She doesn't have an alarm system, does she? Maybe it would be better if she did. Do I need to get arrested to get on the naughty list? Nope. Stop second guessing yourself, Daphne."

I shook my head and checked around the snow covered flower beds for the shop's key. My hand nudged a loose brick, and I quickly snatched the key underneath and unlocked the door. Far too cold to hesitate, I pressed down on the door handle and slipped inside. The soft jingle of the bell betrayed my presence as I tiptoed through the familiar warmth. When no alarm sounded off, I let myself relax enough to breathe in the enticing scent of holiday spices. Daisy closed down the shop for the holiday, but the empty display cases still held the faint scent of delicious baked goods.

Daisy had only opened the shop about a year ago, yet it had already become one of the most popular bakeries in the city and the line was always out the door. I still shuddered thinking of the fight that broke out opening week when she ran out of lava cakes. Now it was as silent as a mouse. The shop was almost eerie without the normal hustle and bustle. I dusted snow from my coat and whispered into the stillness, "Krampus, are you here?"

When no sexy horned creature materialized to ravish me, I tried again. "What kind of naughty criminal breaks into an innocent bakery on Christmas day of all things? Sure hope some supernatural monster man doesn't show up to punish me."

The shop's phone rang and I leapt up with a scream. Heart pounding in my chest, I made my way to the counter and answered it. Hoping it was my monster man and not like…the police. "Hello?"

It was neither Krampus nor the cops, but Daisy. Her tone was clipped as she asked, "Why are you in my shop?"

Chapter 3

"Oh, hi Daisy!"

"Hello," she answered in a measured tone. "You're in my shop."

"Why...yes," I said, leaning against the counter. I looked around for the security camera, mentally kicking myself for forgetting to check for one. "It would appear that I am."

"Why are you in my shop, leaning against my pristine counters?"

I stood, quickly brushing bits of snow off the wood. "Well, there's a good explanation for that really."

"Oh, really?"

"Yes really. You see, I am starting a...new Christmas tradition! Yeah, that's it, a new Christmas tradition where I break into my friend's shop and steal-" I looked around the empty display cases. Shit. "Nothing. Just a fun little game where I test how well your camera works."

I didn't need to see her to know she was pinching the bridge of her nose on the other end of the phone. "Daphne, tell me this has nothing to do with Louis."

"Hell no. He can rot. I'm done with him."

"Praise be."

I chewed on my lip. "But it is about another man."

"Son of a bitch," she sighed. "Look, just tell me what this has to do with you breaking into my shop."

"Promise you won't laugh."

"You know I won't. Spill it."

"Hey, I'm serious. Remember when you called me freaking out because a demon popped out of your cupcakes or something and I didn't judge you, despite how crazy it sounded? Nor did I judge you when you kept dating that demon?"

"It was the frosting, but continue."

"Right, well, last night I met a demon of my own. But he left before I could ask for his number or scroll or whatever it is you use to talk to Kain. So…"

"So?"

"So I need to get on the naughty list so Krampus comes back and spanks me real good. There. I said it. Happy?"

The phone fell silent, followed by a snort before Daisy burst with laughter. "Krampus? You broke into my shop to get dicked down by evil Santa?"

"He's fucking hot, ok?" I held the phone away from my face to avoid her deafening howls of laughter. "Just for that, I'm gonna rob you for real."

"Wait, wait!" she cried in between giggles. "I'll pull it together, I swear. Ok, phew! Alright, I've got a few hours before I head to my folks for Christmas, catch me up to speed."

I walked around the counter to sit on the stool by the register. My phone buzzed in my pocket, and I pulled it out to see a text from my sister.

* * *

She Who Shall Not Be Named: Hey, mom is pissed you chickened out of dinner. If you're going to be that much of a grinch about Nana's old decrepit house you can just have the damn thing. I'll get the title transferred to you after the holidays. Don't say I never did anything for you.

* * *

Even in defeat, she's still a bitch. I tucked the phone back in

Chapter 3

my pocket, deciding to deal with it later. There were more important matters at hand after all. "Long story short, I broke into Nana's house last night-"

"You're really into the B&E's this week," Daisy interrupted.

"I had good reasons!"

"Did your good reason involve stuffing shrimp in the floorboards? I thought you were joking about that."

"Daisy."

"I'm sorry, you are a beacon of logic and reasoning. Continue."

"As I was saying, I broke in to enact my revenge against Charlotte, but then Krampus showed up to punish me. But, plot twist Daisy, are you ready for this?"

"Edge of my seat, girl."

"He's a man who *listens*."

"Marry him."

"Ok good, now you see what I'm working with. Not only did he listen, he sided with me and helped me scare the ever loving shit out of Louis and Charlotte so they'd abandoned the house. Then he fucked me real good and just left! Just showed me the true meaning of Christmas with his dick and left. Now I'm trying to get back on his naughty list so he comes back. And that's why I broke into your bakery. Which…sorry about that."

"Eh, it's fine. Nothing broken. I don't see any horned Santa's in my shop, though. So I'm guessing it didn't work?"

"No," I said petulantly. "Maybe I should rob a bank or something."

"Follow up question. Instead of turning to a life of crime, have you considered dating apps?"

"Did you have any luck on dating apps before you met Kain?"

There was a pause on the other end, followed by the click of her tongue. "You're right, let's rob a bank."

"Let's? As in we?"

"Hell yes. I need to see where this goes and it gives me an excuse to go home early instead of spending the entire weekend with my extended family. Can we rob Vanguard Holdings down on Kittyhawk street? They're closed all week, along with the other shops in the area." Daisy rambled off a concerning amount of information about the bank's security until I finally interrupted.

"Daisy, bestie, how long have you been planning to rob this bank?"

Her voice took on a light, innocent tone. "Whatever do you mean? I'm just trying to help you."

"You know what, this will go faster if I don't ask questions. See you tomorrow?"

"You got it!"

Chapter 4

Crisp evening air stung my cheeks as I searched the depths of my purse for the keycard to my apartment building. The lack of dexterity in mittens was a real problem, but my hatred for cold fingers outweighed the need for maneuverability. The key card slipped from my hands and plopped into fresh snow. Life is a prison. I let my head rest against the door, forcing the will to live back in my marrow before picking up the card and pressing it to the lock. The green light flashed and I hurried up the stairs into my apartment. Closing the door behind me, I kicked off my heels and hung my purse on the coat rack. "As soon as Charlotte signs over the house, I am breaking this damn lease."

The rumblings of an irritated cat met my ears. I rolled my eyes, already preparing for the old girl's lecture about being left alone. I loved that cat, but damn was she ever dramatic. "Oh don't you grumble at me, Freeloader. You have an automatic feeder. You can survive a night."

There was movement in the living room. I expected it to be

my yowling roommate, but it wasn't. It was Louis. He sat with a bouquet of red roses and a small rectangle box in hand, bathed in the warm glow of the fireplace that crackled with dancing flames.

"Daphne," he said, rising from my couch. His posture was slumped, eyes filled with remorse. "We need to talk."

I crossed my arms, refusing to let the pinpricks at my heart get the better of me. "No, we don't. Nor do I want any gifts from you or whatever the hell this is. You can go ahead and toss those roses into the fireplace on your way out."

He shifted uncomfortably and set his gifts down on the coffee table. Louis held up his hands in surrender, his voice turned soft. "Don't be like that. I know I messed up, but I miss you. Can we try again?"

"Try again after you fucked my sister and gave her my engagement ring? Hmm. Let me think about that for a bit." I put a fist to my chin, pretending to contemplate anything other than his outrageous amount of audacity.

"Daph, don't be cruel, it was an honest mistake. She came onto me and-"

"Oh, you are SO lucky I'm too pretty for prison," I snarled, bitterness welling up inside me. "How did you even get in here? Actually, it doesn't matter." I stepped out of the entryway and motioned to the door. "Get out."

He took a step forward, flinching when Freeloader hissed. I turned to see the old gray tabby perched high in her cat tree next to the balcony, back arched high like she was ready to leap down and claw his face off. Fuck I love that cat.

"I know I messed up, but I miss you."

"Do you miss me, or do you miss the house I'll be inheriting now?"

Chapter 4

His gaze faltered, confirming my suspicions. "Look, Daph, I—"

"Save it, Louis. I don't know why it took me this long to realize you were a hobosexual, but the cats out of the bag. Get out."

He didn't budge. Instead, he reached out and grabbed my arm, pulling me to him. Disgust soured in my mouth and I tried to shove away from him. "Let go of me, Louis!"

"Not until you talk to me!" he barked.

Rage drove my knee into his balls. Louis crumpled to the floor, gasping for air and clutching his injured pride. Freeloader, sensing the tension, leaped down from her perch and arched her back, her fur standing on end as she hissed menacingly at Louis.

I stood over him, my anger still burning hot. I stepped over him to open the door, but he grabbed me by the skirt and yanked me back.

Louis groaned in pain as he stood, then grabbed my wrists before I could shove him away again. "I'm not going anywhere until you listen to what I have to say."

"Dammit Louis, just shut up and listen to me!"

"Don't tell me to shut up!" Louis tightened his grip on my wrists and I winced. The door was just a few feet away and I knew I had to break free. Summoning all the strength I had, I stomped on his foot with my heel, causing him to release his hold momentarily. I pulled away, making a beeline for the door.

My freedom was just within reach when he grabbed a handful of my hair.

Louis dragged me onto the balcony, opened the sliding door and forced me outside. The icy wind stung my skin and the chill bit through my sweater and skirt. I stumbled over to the icy railing, clinging desperately to it as he advanced on me.

Fear gripped my throat at the wild look in his eyes. "What the fuck are you doing? Stop!"

"I just wanted us to talk. But you just have to be a selfish bitch about everything, don't you?" Louis pried my hands from the railing. "If you miss your dead Nan so much, why not pay her a visit?"

I didn't have time to register his words. His hands found my back and the next thing I knew, I was plummeting head first towards the unforgiving pavement. The rushing wind swallowed my scream up. I shut my eyes, bracing for the impact that never came. Instead, I felt myself being lifted against a broad chest covered in a red coat. The scent of evergreen nearly had me jumping for joy. Krampus hooked an arm under my legs and lifted me further against him. A whirlwind of snow surrounded us and I found myself back in my living room. Krampus carried me to the couch without a word.

Louis ran back into the room and his eyes went wide at the sight of my demon. "Wh-what the fuck is that thing?" he stammered.

Krampus's voice was of haunted dreams and the promise of malice. "Louis Meyer Bolton, the charges against you are as follows: racketeering, forced entry, attempted murder," he set me down and pressed a glass into my hand. The lights flickered around him, giving me flashes of Louis's horrified face as he pressed himself against the wall like a trapped animal. The lights continued to flicker erratically, casting eerie shadows that danced across the room.

Louis pressed himself harder against the wall, his eyes widening with fear as Krampus turned to face him. "And finally, touching what's mine."

Chapter 4

I'd say my ears didn't perk up at the last of his words, but it would be a damn lie. I took a sip of the drink in my hand. Did this man just come to my rescue with a caramel snickerdoodle martini? I love him. We're getting married. I'm having his monster babies.

"For these transgressions, you have been placed on my naughty list." The surrounding air seemed to thicken with a palpable sense of dread. Louis tried to stammer out a response, but his voice caught in his throat.

Krampus approached Louis with slow deliberate steps and his long, clawed fingers reached out to grab him. Louis thrashed against some unseen force that bound him, but it was no use. In an instant, Krampus had seized him by the throat, unhooked the sack from his back and stuffed him inside.

As Krampus secured the sack, a chilling wind burst through the chimney, extinguishing the fire in an instant. The hearth emitted an ominous cold, biting at the warmth that lingered in the room. Branches twisted out from the chimney, accompanied by the sounds of sinister laughter. Krampus dragged the struggling sack to the hearth and dropped it amongst the branches. They coiled around it with a gleeful cackle and slithered back up the chimney. The portal closed with a final, ominous snap, and the room returned to an uneasy stillness.

I sipped my drink. "Hot."

My hero snorted, running a hand down his face. "You almost died. You know that, right?"

"I don't think you understand how satisfying it is to see your cheating ex get sacrificed to a cackling chimney portal." I raised my glass in salute. "Thank you, by the way. I don't know if magic Christmas creatures have a rating system but if you do, I'm giving you 5 stars."

His eyes narrowed and he stalked toward me. My heart raced. He loomed over me, his gaze boring into mine. I tried to keep a straight face, but my cheeks were starting to feel warm.

Krampus lowered himself onto the couch, bringing himself dangerously close. His voice was soft and dangerous, "What would you give me as a reward?"

I didn't back down. Instead, I closed the space between us. My lips ghosted his, my hand coming up to caress his cheek. "What would you like, Krampus?"

His clawed fingers tangled themselves in my hair. He leaned forward and nipped my bottom lip. "Everything," he growled.

A thrill went through me. He was asking for me, not just the contract. "Then take me."

He captured my lips with a hunger that mirrored my own. I straddled his hips and tangled my hands in his mane. His tongue teased my lips, and I parted them to give him access. Krampus gripped my ass, pushing my skirt up and grinding his hardened length against me. I moaned into his mouth and his hips bucked in response. He carried me into my bedroom and threw me onto my modest twin mattress. He grabbed me by the hips and held my ass in the air with a single hand. With a lustful growl, he used his other hand to peel my panties up and away from my legs. He looked down at me with a devious smile, then ran that tongue along my thighs. I moaned as the tip got closer to my pussy. He teased me for a minute, licking my hips and cheeks, always coming within an inch of my pussy but never servicing it.

I finally gave in and said "Please, lick me!"

He chuckled deeply, somehow speaking with his tongue out, just like last time "Make me, Daphne."

I cocked my head up at him. For once, there was an invitation

Chapter 4

in his eyes. I slowly hooked my heels behind his horns. Then I tried to pull him. He may as well have been a support beam, because I didn't budge him at all. As I struggled to drag the monster towards my cunt, he finally ran his tongue along my clit. He roughly dragged each of his piercings against me. My legs spasmed uncontrollably as he ran the piercings up and down against my needy clit. I screamed in pleasure, my hips rocking each time a smooth ball of metal ran over my bud. Without realizing it, I had stopped trying to pull the monster down.

"You tried well enough, so I will reward you." Krampus said as he withdrew his tongue. He began to swing it around in circular motions right at my entrance.

When I realized what he was doing, it was already too late: he had bunched his tongue up into a corkscrew. I shook my head and said "No no no no, don't-" but there was no stopping him. He shot his screw-shaped tongue inside me and twisted it around. I came in seconds. I clawed the sheets as he licked me like a soft-bodied drill. Tears formed in my eyes as his piercings pummeled my g-spot. I steadied myself with one hand and reached up with the other. I gripped one of his horns and tried to tug him even closer. This time he let me. His tongue touched parts of me Louis could only dream of. I came again. Krampus steadily slowed down his licking. He pulled his tongue out of me, deliberately running each of his piercings over my clit a final time. He grinned down at me, still holding my hips in the air with a single hand - then he dropped my legs and ass. My vision swam as I occasionally spasmed on the bed for a few minutes.

He put his massive cock in front of my face. It throbbed with intense need.

I realized I hadn't gotten a good look at it the last time. All I could blurt out before he pushed the tip into my mouth was "Why does it look like a candy cane?!" I coughed as Krampus tried to force even half his rod down my throat. I desperately slapped his hips to make him pull back. He groaned and relented a bit. I caught my breath and savored the minty taste of his dick. I swirled my tongue over the red-and-white head and moaned when I tasted his sweet pre-cum and stroked his base with both hands.

"Now take it deep, dear one." he said as he slowly fed me his cock.

I was still coughing as I took him down, but I did my damndest to keep his girth cozy in my throat. Groaning, he balled up my hair in one of his massive fists, then he pulled his hips back further for longer thrusts. I gagged and coughed the whole time, but eventually I felt his dick get even thicker in my mouth.

I started stroking his base faster. He moaned loudly. If I hadn't been falling in love with the monster, his cries would've terrified me. Instead, I sucked his cock all the harder, eager to please the enormous man. He didn't say a word, but I knew what was about to happen when his dick swelled for a final time. With a guttural roar he spilled deep into my throat. I savored each rope of minty sperm against my tongue. I slowed down my jerking and massaged the last bits of cum out of his rod. The scent and smell really put me in the holiday spirit. I pulled his cock out of my mouth and ran my tongue over the tip.

I rested his cockhead against my cheek, "Did I reward you enough, sir?" I asked, batting my eyelashes.

Krampus's jaw fell open. I felt his cock pulse as he grew hard again. He ran a hand down his face before cursing. "You wicked creature, you're going to be the death of me."

Chapter 4

I smiled and kissed the head of his cock. "Is that a n-"
I was on my back before I could even get the words out.

Chapter 5

I awoke as I did most mornings, with Freeloader sitting on my chest, smacking me in the face. I turned my head away, groaning when she yowled in my ear instead of taking the hint. "Alright, fine!"

The cat finally relented when I sat up and left to resume whatever morning ritual cats did when they've ruined their owner's chances of sleeping in. On a holiday no less. I reached a hand to the other side of the bed, seeking Krampus's warmth, only to find the bed empty. I leapt up with a start, looking wildly around the room for any sign of my monster man. "Oh my god, I was so lost in the sauce I still didn't get his fucking number! Ahhh!"

I paced around the room, running my fingers through my disheveled hair as I muttered to myself like the crazy woman I was clearly becoming. "Didn't get his number, didn't put a damn bonnet on. Rookie mistakes, Daphne. Rookie mistakes!"

As I fought the good fight against frizziness, I grabbed my phone and called Daisy. She picked up after a few rings and

Chapter 5

gave a muffled greeting.

"Good, you're up. Listen, I got a bone to pick with that man, so we're headed to the bank as soon as you're ready. Where are you now?"

I heard a slurping straw before she replied. "Hey Sugarplum! Kain and I stopped to grab breakfast. I'm loading his butt in the car and we can be there in ten. You ready for this?" Daisy's voice crackled through the phone. In the background, I could hear her boyfriend Kain's panicked mumblings about her driving. "Well, until you get your license, you can just buckle in and deal with it Mr. Destroyer."

I sighed, pinching the bridge of my nose. "More than ready. Get this, Krampus came again last night, spent the entire night with me, then just vanished before I woke up. Like who does that?"

"Men," she said simply. There was an indignant grumble in the background, but she ignored him. "So, are we still doing this or are you giving up on him?"

"Hell no! He owes me an explanation at least. We're robbing the damn bank!"

"Excellent. Am I picking you up or are you meeting us there?"

"Seeing as it's literally three blocks away from me and I don't want to die, I'll meet you there."

"Oh hush, the both of you. I'm a damn excellent driver!" Kain broke out in laughter and I hung up before I got sucked into an argument on whether her lead foot was a danger to us all. It was.

I stormed out of my apartment, a woman on a mission. The morning streets were unusually quiet. Christmas decorations adorned the closed shops, their festive jolly colors almost mocking me with their cheer. As I approached the bank, Daisy's car pulled up and she jumped out with a wide grin and a brick in hand.

"Ready to fuck up the establishment?" she asked.

Kain emerged from the passenger side. His red skin matched the decorative Santa blow-up doll next to the bank's entrance. "What did I say about swinging that around before I cloaked the area?"

Daisy tucked the brick behind her back and gave him a wide smile.

The demon shook his head, unamused. "It's like you want to get arrested." Kain snapped his fingers, then gestured to the bank. "Alright, shields up. Do your worst."

"Shield?" I asked.

Daisy beamed at her man in pride. "I told Kain to use his demon magic to shroud the area in an illusion. Any non magical creature outside a forty-foot radius of the bank won't be able to see us."

"Oh. Well damn, that's convenient."

"I know, I'm magnificent," Kain said.

"Humble, too," Daisy teased.

The demon rolled his eyes and took a seat in the car. "I'll keep watch, you ladies continue your debauchery."

I nodded, my frustration fueling the fire within me. The locked bank doors loomed in front of me, its windows reflecting my actions back at me. My eyes looked wild, but somehow my silk press remained immaculate. Good, at least I'd look pretty for my mug shot if things went south.

Daisy stepped beside me and looked from me to the door. "So, are we doing this or are we just checking ourselves out?" She struck a pose, then turned around to twerk at her reflection.

I snorted, laughter bubbling through my determination.

Chapter 5

"Dammit Daisy, I'm trying to focus."

"Breaking and entering *again*, Daphne? You truly are a glutton for punishment."

I turned to see Krampus standing there, holding two steaming cups of coffee. Surprise momentarily replaced my anger and confusion.

"Krampus! Where the hell have you been?" I demanded, my hands on my hips.

He shrugged, handing me a cup of coffee. "I went to grab us some coffee. You were gone when I returned."

Embarrassment colored my cheeks. "Oh…"

"Daphne?" Daisy called behind me. "How long did you wait before you flew off the handle?"

"I…that's not important."

Daisy snorted.

"Is that why you're here now, my dear one?" Krampus asked, a small smirk teasing his lips. At my glare, he laughed and pulled me closer to whisper in my ear. "You know, you don't need to get on the naughty list for another taste of my claws. You've learned the bed prettily enough."

I reached up, grabbed him by the horn and kissed him, enjoying the taste of coffee on his lips. "Oh no, that's twice you've left me to wake up alone." I ran a finger up his neck, relishing the shiver that wracked his body. "Today you're going to be the one on your knees."

His gaze heated. "Don't make promises you can't keep, dear one."

Crash!

We looked to see that Daisy had thrown her brick through the bank's window. Glass shattered into a million pieces and littered the sidewalk. Daisy let out a triumphant yell and flipped off the bank. "That's for not approving my small business loan!" she screamed, grinning.

Krampus clicked his tongue as he eyed the mess. "You know what? I'm off the clock."

As the alarm blared in the background, we hastily retreated, leaving the scene of our "crime." Our laughter echoed through the empty streets, a peculiar end to a Christmas adventure that I wouldn't soon forget.

About the Author

Kimberly Lemming is on an eternal quest to avoid her calling as a main character. She can be found giving the slip to that new werewolf that just blew into town and refusing to make eye contact with a prince of a far-off land. Dodging aliens looking for Earth booty can really take up a girl's time.

But when she's not running from fate, she can be found writing diverse fantasy romance. Or just shoveling chocolate in her maw until she passes out on the couch.

You can connect with me on:
- https://www.kimberlylemming.com
- https://twitter.com/KimberlyLemming
- https://www.facebook.com/KimberlyLemming
- https://www.instagram.com/kimberlylemming
- https://www.tiktok.com/@kimberlylemming

Subscribe to my newsletter:
- https://www.kimberlylemming.com/newsletter

Also by Kimberly Lemming

That Time I Got Drunk And Saved A Demon: Mead Mishaps Book 1
All I wanted to do was live my life in peace. Maybe get a cat, expand my spice farm. Really, anything that doesn't involve going on a quest where an orc might rip my face off. But they say the Goddess has favorites. If so, I'm clearly not one of them.

After saving the demon Fallon in a wine-drunk stupor, all he wanted to do was kill an evil witch enslaving his people.

I mean, I get it, don't get me wrong. But he's dragging me along for the ride, and I'm kind of peeved about it. On the bright side, he keeps burning off his shirt.

That Time I Got Drunk And Yeeted A Love Potion At A Werewolf: Mead Mishaps Book 2

Anyone else ever thrown a drink at someone's head, only to miss entirely and hit a stranger behind them? Then have that stranger fall madly in love with you because it turned out that drink you threw was a love potion? No, just me? Well damn.

Dealing with a pirate ship full of demons that just moved into town was hard enough. Now on top of it, I have to convince a werewolf that I'm not his fated mate, he's just drugged. Easier said than done.

Though I have to say, having a gorgeous man show up and do all of your chores while telling you you're beautiful isn't the worst thing to happen to a girl.

That Time I Drunk and Saved A Human: Mead Mishaps Book 3

When I was a little girl, my ma used to read me stories every night. Some were epic adventures with high stakes and exciting twists while others were of princesses trapped in towers guarded by fierce dragons. The pitiful princess would be stuck inside all day pining for her prince charming to come and rescue her. I always hated those stories. I couldn't imagine why the lazy thing didn't just get up and leave. Ironic since I was now stuck in that same situation. Turns out, when a dragon holds you hostage, he doesn't just let you get up and leave.

Who knew?

Just when I thought I saw hope on the horizon, that hope was smashed to bits by-you guessed it-another damn dragon.

Mistlefoe: A Mead Realm Tale

It's all fun and games until someone catches feelings

Fate sends me straight into the lion's den. Or rather, the fox's den. After my dad trespassed into a powerful fox demon's territory, our family is struck with a powerful curse. Now, to remove it, I'll have to appeal to the demon's better nature.

Easier said than done. That arrogant fox demon won't be swayed by an apology basket full of treats. He does, however, need a fake mate for a week-long Winter Festival.

Though I'd be a liar if I didn't admit that our doting lovers' act was becoming harder by the day. The more time I spent with Lucca, the more his irresistible charms get under my skin. Deep down, I know it's all a game. But my heart just can't seem to get the memo. When our week-long affair comes to a close, will I really be able to walk away?

A Bump In Boohail: A Mead Realm Tale

Samhain was the biggest festival of the year. It was the time that the veil between our world and the otherworld thinned, meaning any manner of spirits could come through and wreak havoc. Not that I had anything to worry about with a dragon at my side. This year the festival would be the perfect excuse to snuggle up with my partner and enjoy Fall in full swing. Or at least it would have been, if I could find him.

This is a short story set in the Mead Mishaps series featuring Cinnamon and Fallon and is not a stand alone. It should be read after That Time I Got Drunk And Yeeted A Love Potion At A Werewolf.

Two Scoops Of Hellfire

It took about two weeks into the pandemic lockdown before I went stark raving mad. In a bold attempt at a new skill, I decided to give baking a try. However, I took to the new venture like a fish to astrophysics and ended up with a battle demon in my kitchen.

Figures.

Will Kain The Destroyer end my life, or end my everlasting boredom?

It's an Erotica. Take a wild guess.

Printed in the USA
CPSIA information can be obtained
at www.ICGtesting.com
LVHW021604201024
794324LV00003B/276